Secret Witch

Robina Beckles Willson

Illustrated by Azalea Sturdy

This edition produced exclusively for

WHSMITH

The witch was worn out. It was wet and
windy. She was cold and cross. Her cat
was bedraggled. Her toad was dripping.

'We'll land on this roof,' she shouted.
But, as she landed, her broomstick was
caught in a chimney. 'Haven't you two
enough magic between you to guide me
safely?' the witch complained. 'I fly you
everywhere, then you let me crash land.
Now we're stuck.'

The cat said nothing, but began to climb down the chimney in to the sloping roof. The witch and toad followed. By a trap door the toad began puffing himself up.

'Magic not strong enough?' asked the witch, snapping her fingers to make the door open. She felt better when it opened. They looked down and saw a box lift with wooden doors.

'Bring me what's left of my broom-stick,' the witch ordered the cat. 'Then we can explore. We need somewhere to live for the rest of the winter.'

The cat jumped down beside the box. The witch slid down her broomstick, with the toad on her shoulder. Then she snapped her fingers. But the wooden doors stayed shut. The witch tugged furiously at the doors, which flew open. 'Clever me,' said the witch. Then she saw metal gates as well. 'Your turn now, you useless two,' shouted the witch.

The cat climbed up on a shelf, with the toad on his back. He leaned over to see if he could claw the lift gates open. The toad pushed at the side of the gates and pressed a button there. Slowly the gates slid open.

'Perhaps you've picked up a bit of magic from me after all,' said the witch, stepping inside and looking at all the buttons on the wall. 'You can come too, I suppose.'

When she pressed a button the doors
shut again, and the lift began to move
slowly downward.

'Not bad magic,' said the witch. 'A
flying house. Warmer than a flying
broomstick, don't you think?'

The lift stopped. The witch pressed
another button and it started again.

Each time she pressed a button the gates
opened or shut or the lift moved up or
down. When the lift stopped they opened
the doors and peered out at each floor of
the building.

   They rode up and down the tall building
until they were too tired even to press a
button. Then they all fell asleep.

8

The next morning, Mr Mib, the caretaker, came to open up the building. He picked up the letters to take them to the four floors in the building. Mr Mib loved riding in the lift by himself. But then he saw the doors open and the lift ropes hanging down.

'Gracious heavens!' cried Mr Mib. 'What's happened to my lift?'

He started to stump upstairs, hotter and crosser with every step he took, right to the top of the building.

There he saw the lift at last, with the gates and doors shut. He pulled back the gates and pressed the button. The doors opened.

'What are you doing in my house?' asked the witch.

'This is my lift, not a house,' he said. 'People don't live in lifts.'

'If it's yours, we've come to stay with you for the winter. My two familiar friends and me.'

'I *thought* I smelt fish,' said Mr Mib.

'A cat must eat,' said the witch. 'We were out at a Hallowe'en party and he was hungry.'

'But how did you get into the lift?' asked Mr Mib.

'We got stuck in the chimney and climbed down. These magic doors make almost as good magic as mine.'

'Don't try any magic now,' said Mr Mib quickly. 'People use this lift every day for going up and down to their offices. You can't stay.'

'You couldn't throw us out to shiver all winter. Poor pussy might die of cold. Your people could share the lift with us. We could have it at night, and they have it in the day. We usually sleep in the daytime.'

'We couldn't have toads and cats and witches in the building. The boss wouldn't like it.'

'One toad. One cat. And one witch only would stay in the roof,' said the witch. 'I could fly the lift all night. And by spring, you could have mended my broomstick.'

'Are you out to bewitch the building and me? Anything else you want?' asked Mr Mib.

'We shall need fish and milk every day for Cat. And some chocolate for me. Toad will eat all your flies and spiders in this old building. We'll be a great help.'

'I wonder?' said Mr Mib. 'But you'll have to hide before everybody comes to work.'

'You have been lucky even to meet us,' said the witch, snapping her fingers angrily, as they vanished.

'Perhaps I've been seeing things,' said Mr Mib.

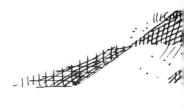

But all through the day he kept smelling fish. When he had a cup of tea with the tea-lady she said: 'I don't know about you, Mr Mib, but I think there's a whiff of fish in this building today. Most of all in the lift.'

'I'll see it has a good clean out tomorrow,' said Mr Mib.

But when Mr Mib came to work the next morning, the lift had gone. Even on the top floor, he only saw the ropes dangling down.

Downstairs, people were waiting in the hall.

'Oh, there you are, Mib,' said the boss. 'The lift seems rather slow this morning.'

'It does,' said Mr Mib. 'Not like my lift at all.'

'I'm tired of waiting,' said one young man. 'I'm going to jog to the top.'

'Find the lift and send it down here,'
ordered the boss.

But still the lift did not come.

'Mr Mib. Where is that lift?'

'It seems to have gone, sir.'

'Gone! Lifts do not go up into thin air,
my man.'

'This one has. I wonder if I'll ever see it
again,' said Mr Mib sadly.

'Rubbish,' shouted the boss. 'Someone
has left the gates open; fooling around. Just
find it.'

All that day Mr Mib missed his lift.
People grumbled up and down stairs.

He was glad when people began to leave. He
was just going home himself when he saw
a black tail sliding down the banister. Next
moment, the lift came down. He rushed
to the gates. Inside he heard stamping:
'Which button, you stupid Toad?'

'The bottom one,' shouted Mr Mib.

The doors opened and the witch dashed
out. 'That wasn't fair,' she told the cat.
'You didn't really win! Toad pressed the
wrong button.'

The cat yowled and arched his back.

'No fish for you then,' said the witch. 'Is
our food ready?'

'No, it is *not*,' said Mr Mib. 'Where have
you been all day?'

'Sleeping in the roof, just as we said.'

'But where was the lift?'

'I squeezed it up with us.'

'But Witch,' said Mr Mib. 'That won't do. I told you. We *need* the lift.'

'Nobody saw us,' said the witch sulkily.

'Nobody saw the lift either. Look, I'll show you. This is the ground floor. I have my cubby hole here. Parcels are packed here, and letters collected. This kitchen is where the tea-lady makes tea and coffee, so that she can take it to the offices.'

'In my lift?'

'In the building's lift. Come on up.'

They went in the lift, and Mr Mib showed the witch the telephone switchboard, then the offices and cloakrooms on the first, second and third floors.

'It's all boring tables and chairs,' said the witch. 'We'll keep you company on the days nobody else comes but you. I've seen, flying over the place.'

'Those are Sundays and holidays, when I check the building,' said Mr Mib.

'We could have fast rides in the lift together. Right through the roof if you like.'

'I wouldn't want the lift damaged.'

'Magic makes things better. I could make the lift sing.'

'No thank you,' said Mr Mib. 'Though I wouldn't mind a song myself, of a Sunday. But on office work days you must be a secret.'

'A secret witch. I might like that,' said the witch.

'And no more taking the lift away,' said Mr Mib.

'I shall have to take it shopping if we don't get any food,' the witch reminded him.

'I have a bit of chocolate and fish in my cubby hole.'

They all went in and the witch said: 'That *was* a bit of chocolate.'

'I'll bring you more tomorrow. I'm

going home for my supper now,' Mr Mib
told her.

'We'll look after the building,' said the
witch.

'Goodnight,' said Mr Mib.

The next morning, Mr Mib was pleased
to see the lift in its usual place.

'Well done, Mib,' said the boss, when he
came in. 'Stuck somewhere, was it?'

'In a way, sir,' said Mr Mib.

Just then a man came running out of the
parcels room. 'Come and see this,' he
called to Mr Mib.

There were black paw marks on every
parcel and letter there.

'A wild animal has been stamping on my
ink pad,' said the man.

'Not a big one,' said Mr Mib.

'It's a big mess.'

'Oh dear,' said Mr Mib.

As he went along the hall he saw a strange person, wearing wellingtons, a long man's coat and a lady's fluffy hat.

'Oh heavens, who is that?' thought Mr Mib.

On the first floor, people were looking
at a high tower of wastepaper bins.

'Who's done this? Have the cleaners
gone mad?' asked one lady.

Mr Mib went to the other offices, wondering what he would see next.

It was the strange person, holding an umbrella. When she saw Mr Mib, she slid down to the floor below.

'I know who that is. Witch being secret. What else has she done?'

He found out in the next office. All the flowers were upside down in their vases.

'Mr Mib. Did you ever?' said the secretary. 'You know violets drink through their heads? I had my violets drinking like that overnight. And someone's been and put *all* the flowers upside down. Drips everywhere. It's no joke.'

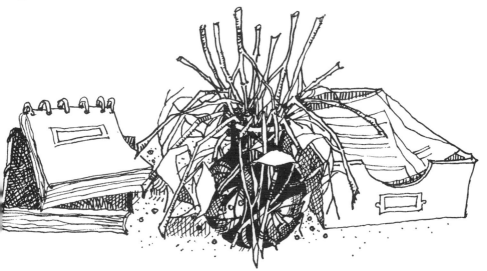

Just then her 'phone started ringing and Mr Mib hurried away. But he met the boss who said: 'Mib. The lift stinks of fish. See to it, please. And my 'phone keeps buzzing. Tell the girl at the switchboard.'

On the way, Mr Mib saw the strange person, wearing a fur coat and a man's hat, but she ran away too fast for him to catch her.

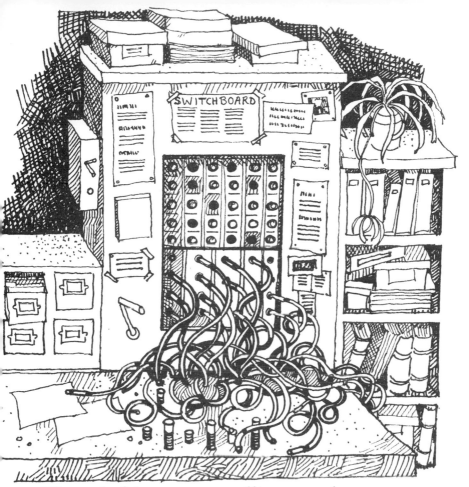

The witch's cat was pulling out the
switchboard's cords, but she ran away
when Mr Mib came in.

'What was that?' called the girl. 'I was
only out of the room a minute.'

'I couldn't be sure,' said Mr Mib. 'The
boss said his 'phone has been buzzing.'

'I should think so. Look at all those,' said
the girl. 'What a tangle.'

'I think I need a cup of tea,' Mr Mib said
to himself. But in the kitchen, the tea-lady
said:

'Just look at the boss's biscuits!
Someone's been nibbling them. Who
could have . . . .'

Then she screamed and jumped on a chair. 'There's an animal been at them. I saw him. He's up in the corner.'

'Just a mouse, I expect,' said Mr Mib soothingly.

'Too big,' she shrieked. 'It might be a rat. Horrible thing. Send it away.'

Mr Mib knew only too well who the animal was. 'Go away,' he said.

'Has he gone?' asked the tea-lady
nervously. 'You are brave, Mr Mib. Have
a cup of tea.'

But the tea didn't make Mr Mib feel any
better. He saw the strange person again, in
a leather jacket and motorbike helmet.

'I'll have to deal with that witch
tonight,' he said to himself. When
everybody else had gone home he found
her.

'I told you to be a secret witch.'

'I was. Nobody knew me. I found
dressing-up things in all those
cloakrooms. Didn't you think I had good
disguises?' said the witch.

'No. And Cat made black marks and
fiddled with the 'phones. And Toad
nibbled biscuits.'

'He was just tasting. He didn't like them, did you, Toad? Spiders are much juicier.'

'Never mind spiders,' said Mr Mib. 'You three must *not* be seen. Or I'll send you away.'

'But it's fun for you having us here,' said the witch. 'Come on, I'm still not tired. Let's have a race without the lift.'

'Only if you promise not to go into the offices, night or day,' said Mr Mib.

'If we can use the lift and your cubby-hole when you've gone home. That's fair,' said the witch.

'Oh all right,' said Mr Mib. 'I'll leave your food there. Now just one race.'

'You have the banister and I'll have my broomstick this time,' said the witch. 'I'll beat you.'

And she did. But Mr Mib found that he quite liked sliding down the banisters when no-one else was in the building. Except the witch and Toad and Cat.

Everything worked well all through
November. But in December people
began to stay late to pin up Christmas
cards. Some clambered up on office stools
to hang streamers. Others dangled big
bunches of mistletoe over their doorways.

'That's a magic plant,' said the witch.
'Why have they hung it up?'

'It's an old custom, to catch people and kiss them under the mistletoe,' explained Mr Mib.

'I like that idea,' said the witch.

'It's only at Christmas,' he said quickly.

'We'll enjoy Christmas here. I expect there'll be a party.'

'Just for the staff in the offices,' Mr Mib told her.

'Not you?' demanded the witch. 'They *must* ask you. If not, I'll tell that boss . . . .'

'It's quite all right,' said Mr Mib.

He didn't want the witch to know that he always went to the office party dressed as Father Christmas. Then the witch saw the huge Christmas tree in the hall, decorated with lights and glass balls, and said:

'We must have a good sleep tomorrow, as the party's in the evening, my time.'

'But you're not asked to the party. I'm sorry.'

'You will be if I'm *not* asked to the party,' said the witch. 'And Cat. And Toad.'

'But I can't ask a witch who's not supposed to be here at all.'

'I shan't *be* a witch. I shall be in fancy dress. Like you! I saw your Father Christmas outfit. But now I shan't tell you who I'm going to be.'

The witch deliberately made the lift clang and screech as she went up to the roof.

The next day, Mr Mib was too busy to
worry about the witch. He helped to
arrange plates of food, bottles and glasses.
At seven o'clock, Mr Mib changed in his
cubby-hole, and filled his sack with
parcels.

When he stepped into the hall the
Christmas tree began to sway, then to tip
over slowly.

'Gracious heavens,' exclaimed Mr Mib, as the glass balls jangled on the tree.

'*Now* will you ask me to the party?' said a voice he knew well.

'Witch, where are you?'

'Ask me to the party.'

'All right, come to the party,' said Mr Mib, as the boss hurried into the hall, dressed as a cowboy.

'Now, see here, Mib,' said the boss. 'That tree looks kind of wobbly. Fix it.'

'Certainly sir,' said Mr Mib.

The boss went over to look at the
drinks. The bottles began to clonk and the
glasses to bounce on the table.

'Witch!' Mr Mib exclaimed crossly.

'Which?' said the boss. 'I think I'll take a
glass of wine.'

Trembling, Mr Mib poured a glass of
wine.

'Nervous, Mib?' asked the boss. 'No need. These fancy dress Christmas parties always go well. See here, a bunch of fellows from floor three. We won't know who's who.'

'Maybe I don't want to know who is the witch,' thought Mr Mib.

As the party went on he thought that the
witch had turned herself into a fairy. He
saw a fairy make a jelly wobble off its
plate, a fairy eat the boss's chocolate cake

44

when he wasn't looking, a fairy have three
presents, when everyone else had one from
his sack.

'Good costumes, Mib,' said the boss,
'but there's a funny sort of fairy here. I'm
sure I've never seen her before. Must be
new.'

As he spoke, his cowboy hat blew off
and landed on top of a golden toad on the
Christmas tree.

'Hey!' shouted the boss, and the toad
kicked its legs and sent the hat back.

'NOW THEN,' protested Mr Mib, as
he felt his beard tugged, and he was pulled
to the mistletoe and kissed.

'Perhaps you are better invisible, Witch,' he whispered.

'Oh no I'm not,' said the witch. And a fairy appeared at his side.

'I must be seeing things,' said the boss. 'That fairy came from nowhere. Let's start the carols round the tree, Mib.'

'Now Witch, behave,' murmured Mr Mib. 'You ought to be good if you come to the party.'

'All right,' said the witch, 'if I can sing a solo.'

So Mr Mib began to play his piano accordion. 'The first verse is a solo,' said Mr Mib.

The fairy-witch sang, then everyone joined in. Mr Mib was glad she sang properly, as people were looking puzzled as she stood by him with the butterfly flying round her head.

'Cat always wanted to fly,' she told Mr Mib.

After the carols, people began to go home, but it was very late before the building was empty. Except for Mr Mib. And the witch.

'It was hard work being a fairy,' said the witch.

'Even a bad one!'

'Harder magic being invisible,' said the witch; 'but it was a good party.'

'At least nobody guessed you were a witch,' said Mr Mib.

'I was your Christmas fairy,' said the witch.

For the rest of that winter there was no more trouble in the building. Mr Mib often stayed late to play games with the witch. And, on Christmas day, he brought in a big dinner, which they all enjoyed, except Toad. He ate a juicy spider instead.

Holiday Witch

Robina Beckles Willson

Illustrated by Azalea Sturdy

Mr Mib was singing to the witch, her cat
and her toad. They lived in the lift of the
Building where Mr Mib was caretaker.

'Oh, you'll tak' the high road and I'll tak'
the low road,
    And I'll be in Scotland afore ye.
    But me and my true love will never meet
again
    On the bonnie bonnie banks o' Loch
Lomond.'

'What's a loch mean?'
'Loch is the Scottish name for a lake.'

3

'Sounds good, lots of fish,' said Cat.

'Yes, I'm going fishing when I have my holiday in Scotland,' said Mr Mib.

'I think I need a holiday,' said the witch.

'We'll come too,' said Cat and Toad.

'But I haven't asked any of you,' protested Mr Mib. 'I couldn't take animals on an aeroplane.'

'I could go in your pocket,' said Cat.

4

'And I could go in your other pocket,' added Toad.

'I could fly by broomstick,' said the witch. 'Much faster without a lump of cat on the back. I'll be in Scotland before you, Cat. Or you, Toad. My magic is so much stronger.'

'I'll make a storm come like this if you stop me,' said Cat, clawing at the carpet.

'I shan't stop you,' said the witch. 'I'll race you and get there first.'

'Why don't you three plan some outings together while I'm away?' suggested Mr Mib.

'No. You might need me. And I need a holiday,' said the witch. 'Now, let's learn your Scottish song. Play the tune on your piano accordion and we'll join in.'

Cat yowled, Toad grunted and the witch sang 'Loch Lomond' with Mr Mib.

6

He did not think that the witch or Cat
or Toad could manage the journey all the
way from London to Scotland. So he
soon said goodbye and went home. But
he did not know that the witch, Cat and
Toad were following him, to see where
he lived.

When Mr Mib set off the next morning
he was carrying a black case, a long bag
carrying his fishing rod, and a plastic bag.
As he walked down the street to the
station he did not see the witch creeping
behind. And the witch did not see Cat,
and Cat did not see Toad.

While Mr Mib was buying his ticket the
plastic bag tipped over. But he did not see
why.

Mr Mib got into the train and sat
down. 'It will be a real rest in Scotland,'
he thought. And he did not see a
broomstick on the luggage rack or what
was behind his case.

At the airport, there were magic sliding doors which opened when Mr Mib stood in front of them. 'The witch would like those,' he thought. And he did not see her follow him in.

'First I must take my luggage to be weighed,' said Mr Mib.

He put the case and long bag on the scales. 'I'll keep this plastic bag with me.'

'They're not too heavy,' said the lady. 'Is there a fishing rod in that bag?'

'Yes, it's my first visit to Scotland, and I hope to catch a lot of fish in the lochs there.'

'Bring one back for me,' said the lady. And she did not see Cat jump on to the moving belt by Mr Mib's case.

Mr Mib thought he had time to have
something to eat before he flew to
Scotland. He went to the airport café and
bought a sandwich, a chocolate biscuit
and a cup of tea. Lots of people were
waiting for their aeroplanes, and he
watched them as he ate and drank. So he
did not see someone lean over and take his
chocolate biscuit.

'Oh dear,' said Mr Mib, when he saw his empty plate. 'I must be more excited than I knew. I thought I had bought a chocolate biscuit.'

Just then a voice called over the loudspeaker: 'Passengers for flight BA 979 to Edinburgh, Scotland, please go to Gate 3.'

'That's me,' said Mr Mib, and hurried out to a doorway called Gate 3. He showed his ticket and went into a waiting room. There were so many people that he did not see what was propped up in the corner.

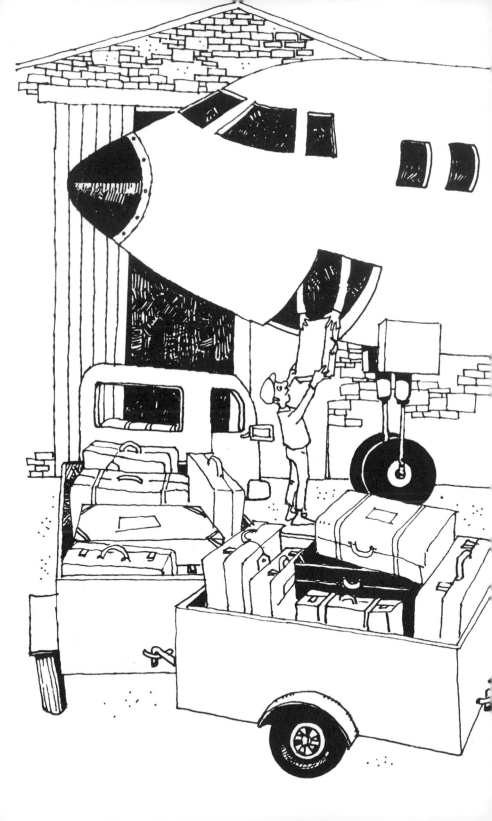

Soon they all went outside on to the tarmac and walked over to a big aeroplane. A luggage truck was being unloaded into the hold. Mr Mib could not spot his black case. He walked up the steps into the aeroplane. The air-hostess at the doorway said to the pilot: 'There's a funny old broom left here. What shall I do with it?'

'Leave it behind,' he answered. 'It can go in the truck to lost property.'

She came back up the steps and shut the door.

The broomstick did not stay in the truck. As the aeroplane's engines began to warm up, the broomstick rose in the air and landed on the aeroplane's tail, sliding about when it began to roll along the runway.

Inside the aeroplane Mr Mib sat in his comfortable seat.

'Fasten your seat belts, please,' said the air-hostess.

Mr Mib looked out of the window as the aeroplane began to rise into the air with a roaring noise. So he did not hear an angry voice shouting on the aeroplane's tail, nor some yowling down below. He saw the land so far away that the houses looked like boxes and the cars like toys.

'We're going so fast I'll soon be in Scotland,' thought Mr Mib. 'Time for a little read.' He put his hand into his bag to find his paper and felt something clammy.

'Oh dear,' said Mr Mib. 'I hope I'm wrong, but I think I know what's there.' He had a quick look and whispered: 'Down, Toad, down.'

'But I want to see,' hissed Toad; 'then I can tell the witch and Cat about it. I've never been in an aeroplane before.'

'You'll be thrown off if you're caught,' Mr Mib told him. 'Keep out of sight. The lady by me may hate toads.'

'How could anyone hate me?' asked Toad; but he kept well down in the bag and peeped out with just one eye when the air-hostess brought the passengers drinks on a trolley.

'I'm a bit thirsty too,' he whispered.

'You'll have to wait,' Mr Mib told him. 'Have a drink when we get there.'

'Please keep your seat-belts on,' said the captain over the loud-speaker. 'We are running into some turbulence, perhaps a little local storm, and it may be just a bit bumpy.'

'Cat can make storms,' said Toad.

'Cat is miles away in London,' said Mr Mib. 'It's just a little thunderstorm in the air. A Toad wouldn't understand.'

'I'd have a good guess he's clawing about somewhere,' muttered Toad to himself.

The aeroplane flew more smoothly in puffy white clouds, and Mr Mib began to enjoy his journey.

'This is your captain speaking,' said the pilot. 'You may unfasten your seat-belts. We have passed through that patch of turbulence. It is fine and sunny in Edinburgh, and we hope to land in half an hour.'

The rest of the journey went quickly. 'I hope you have enjoyed your flight with us,' said the air-hostess over the loud-speaker. 'Please fasten your seat-belts again. We are going to land in Edinburgh in a few minutes.'

The aeroplane began to turn downwards. Mr Mib held his breath and hoped they would not land with a bang as he saw the ground getting nearer and nearer. But the wheels came out of the aeroplane's body at the right moment. It landed neatly and rolled along big runways before at last it stopped.

'Well, here I am in bonnie Scotland,'
murmured Mr Mib.

'Please check you have all your hand
luggage with you,' said the air-hostess.

'Me too,' whispered Toad, peeping out
and being pushed back by Mr Mib.

At the doorway of the aeroplane the
pilot was talking to the air-hostess.

'It was an odd flight,' he said. 'We kept
thinking there was something on the tail.
Then it went away. And we weren't
expecting that little storm either.'

'Never mind,' said the air-hostess.
'We're here safe and sound.'

Mr Mib said goodbye and was glad they could not see the odd hand luggage he was carrying. They might not care for a Toad as a passenger. He walked down the steps of the aeroplane. Already the bags were being unloaded on to a truck. Mr Mib hoped that his bags had arrived safe and sound too. He walked over the tarmac into a big hall.

Moving belts were shunting bags and cases from a shute. Mr Mib waited for a long time as the luggage began to move slowly round and round.

Mr Mib saw his fishing bag, and picked it off the moving belt. 'All I need now is my case.'

But when that came along so did Cat.

When he saw Mr Mib he jumped off.

'I've won the race,' he cried. 'I hope there's a prize, Mr Mib. I'm the winner.'

'Oh no you're not,' said the witch, suddenly appearing. 'I've been here all the time, while you dawdled along that slow belt. I flew here.'

'But how?' asked Mr Mib.

'By broomstick, of course,' the witch told him.

'But you couldn't fly as fast as my aeroplane,' said Mr Mib.

'Well, I did sit on the tail of the aeroplane sometimes,' admitted the witch. 'But I didn't like it much. Too wet and windy.'

Cat laughed. 'That was me, raising a storm. I didn't like it much shut in down there, even if I was warm and dry.'

'You cheated in the race, while I flew bravely along on my broomstick,' said the witch. 'And I was here with Mr Mib first.'

24

'Oh no you weren't,' shouted Toad, jumping out of Mr Mib's bag. 'I was here first, because I came inside the cabin with Mr Mib.'

'That's not racing,' said the witch. 'Just sitting there.'

'Oh yes it is,' said Toad and Cat.

'You cheated, I expect, being invisible,' said Cat. So it was not hard hiding.'

'You're just not clever enough at magic,' said the witch. 'I can always see your tail sticking up, when you think you're invisible.'

They made such a noise arguing that people began to stare. Mr Mib sighed: 'I wish I'd stayed at home for a bit of peace.'

'Now then. What's all this about?' asked a policeman, coming along. 'Seems to be a bit of a disturbance with you and your friends, sir.'

'I don't know that they are friends,' said Mr Mib helplessly.

'Cat's a cheat,' said the witch, stepping on his tail. 'Don't you scratch me either!'

arrivals

'Madam,' said the policeman. 'We can't
have fights in the airport, you know. I
must ask you. . . .'

But as he spoke the witch vanished.
And the policeman found himself talking
to a laughing Toad.

'Take no notice of her,' said Toad. 'She just hates losing a race.'

'Oh no I didn't,' shouted the witch, appearing again.

'Now Witch. And Cat. And Toad,' said Mr Mib. 'If you don't all behave I shall ask the policeman to send you straight back to England.'

'He couldn't do that. We've come on holiday with you, to keep you company,' said the witch.

'I can't say you were asked. But now you're here you'll have to count it that all three won the race. If you're staying with me, you've got to be friends.'

'All right, I suppose,' said the witch.

'All right,' said Toad and Cat.

'We don't have many visitors like you,' said the policeman. 'So I shall have my eye on you, that you do behave.'

'Thank you,' said Mr Mib. 'Now I'm here I shall hope to go fishing.'

'Lots of fresh fish for me,' said Cat.

★   ★   ★

The next morning, they left the hotel to go fishing. But on the way they passed a Scottish shop.

'As I'm in Scotland I think I should wear a kilt,' said the witch, and led the way in.

Mr Mib had to follow. The witch

the scotch shop

began to try on tartan hats. Then she
found a tartan umbrella and a tartan bag.

'What lovely things for you to buy for
us, Mr Mib,' she said.

30

'They cost a lot,' said Mr Mib. 'Just one thing each.'

'I think Cat has chosen his,' said the witch.

'This is a fierce furry thing, not a present,' said Cat, his fur standing up spikily as he pounced.

Mr Mib hurried over to him. 'You mustn't bite things in the shop. That's not alive, Cat. It's a seal-skin sporran, a sort of pouch people wear on their kilts.'

'I'm sure it squeaked,' said Cat.

'That was me,' said Toad. 'To frighten
this animal on the wall. Just look at his
horns, Mr Mib. Now that is a real
animal.'

'It's only a stuffed deer's head with
antlers. No need to get puffed up, Toad.
It won't hurt you. It's not alive either.
Come away and look at the clothes. I like
those velvet jackets with silver buttons,
but they cost too much money.'

'I think you'd better buy my kilt first,'

said the witch. 'I could have this matching cloak and hat.'

'I said *one* thing each,' Mr Mib told her. 'Put those back.'

In the end, Toad chose a tartan scarf and Cat a fluffy tam-o-shanter. Mr Mib and the witch each had a kilt.

'Perhaps we'll come back tomorrow for some more things,' said the witch.

'Only if *you* have a lot of money to spend,' said Mr Mib. 'We are going to the loch now.'

They walked there, looking very smart in their tartan clothes.

Mr Mib sat fishing for a long time. Witch was helping Toad to find spiders.

'I thought you'd catch millions of fish in this big loch. It's boring just waiting,' said Cat. He began to scratch at Mr Mib's kilt.

A grey cloud appeared in the sky. The loch was all grey until something black moved under the water.

'I've got a catch,' said Mr Mib. He began to wind in his fishing line.

'It's heavy. Lend a paw, Cat, if you want a big fish,' called Mr Mib.

The line was jerking. 'It's too much for us. Witch, come and help land this giant fish before it pulls me in the water!'

The witch held Cat. And Cat held Mr Mib, pulling hard.

'It will break the line,' gasped Mr Mib. 'We'll have to let it go.'

'I'll help,' said Toad. 'I'm strong, full of Scottish spiders.'

They tugged at the line. Slowly,

something black came out of the water. It
was not a fish. It was a monster from the
loch.

'Gracious heavens,' cried Mr Mib,
when the monster showed big teeth and
caught Toad in his claws.

'I only wanted a fish,' whimpered Cat,
hiding behind Mr Mib.

'Put that Toad down,' ordered the witch, 'or I'll turn you into a tiddler.'

'Oh Witch, do you think you could? He's so huge,' whispered Mr Mib.

'I'll try,' she said.

'I don't come out of my loch for nothing,' bellowed the monster. 'And I don't fancy fur to eat, like that scraggy cat. A toad might taste better.'

'That Cat is magic. But I'm more magic,' said the witch, sitting on her broomstick. 'Let Toad go.'

'Shan't,' said the monster.

'Oh yes you will,' said the witch.

Slowly the monster began to shrink until he was not much bigger than Mr Mib.

'Now will you drop that Toad?' asked Mr Mib.

'No I won't,' said the monster.

'I can't make him any smaller,' said the witch. 'He's too big to push in the water.'

'We must get rid of him somehow,' said Mr Mib. 'What will you take to give us back our friend Toad?'

'I want that cat's hat,' said the monster. 'And a special treat.'

'Cat, please will you give him your hat?' asked Mr Mib, wondering what would be a special treat for a monster.

'I'll give you the special treat,' said the witch. 'A ride on my broomstick.'

'But he might bite you,' said Cat, trembling.

44

'He wouldn't dare,' said the witch.
'Hop on behind.'

The monster dropped Toad, who jumped into Mr Mib's pocket. Then the monster clambered on to the broomstick.

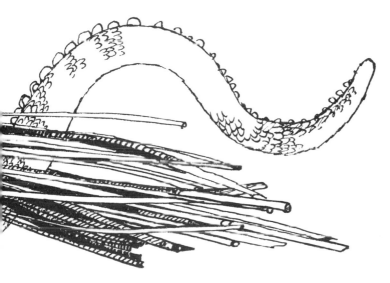

Slowly they rose into the air. Then the witch began to fly round and round the loch. She whirled in circles faster and faster until . . .

SPLASH! The witch had tipped her broomstick downwards, and the monster back into the loch.

When she landed again by Mr Mib she said:

'You see, you couldn't manage without me.'

'Not really, nor could Cat or Toad,' admitted Mr Mib. 'Let's go back to the hotel. I'll *buy* some fish for Cat.'

'And some chocolate for me,' added the witch.

'You were even braver with the monster than you were in the race,' said Toad, grateful to be free.

'I'm even glad you won the race,' added Cat.

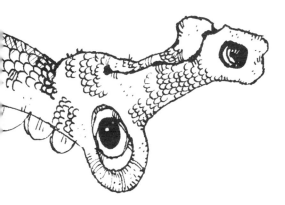

After that, the holiday went well, with no more monsters. At a hotel party, the witch sang 'Loch Lomond'. Then she danced to bagpipe music with Mr Mib. He thought that he would like to try playing the bagpipe.

Mr Mib was pleased after all that the witch, Cat and Toad had raced up to Scotland to keep him company.

GRIMBLEGRAW AND
THE WUTHERING WITCH

GRIMBLEGRAW AND THE WUTHERING WITCH

Barbara Sleigh

Pictures by Glenys Ambrus

For Ben

'Girls!' said Prince Benedict scornfully.
'Simpering, giggling, feather-brained
creatures. Especially princesses. And now
I've got to marry one I've never seen!'

'Dear me,' said the Gentleman of the
Bed-chamber. 'I am sure that does not
describe the charming young princess
who even now may be waiting to meet
you. If I could suggest that the royal right
leg might be raised a little higher, so that I
can put on the other silk stocking?'

5

'Oh, bother the other silk stocking!' grumbled the Prince. 'And bother princesses, all the lot of them!' And he jumped to his feet and ran from the room.

Once in the closet next door, he changed his scarlet velvet tunic for one of sober green, slung his legs over the window-sill, and climbed down the ivy that grew outside, with an ease that suggested it was not for the first time.

'Boys!' said Princess Yolanda, in
another palace, not far away. 'Boring,
bossy, boastful creatures. And I've come
all this way, in a jolting coach, just to be
married to one!'

'For shame!' said her old nurse. 'Such a
handsome young man as they say he is!
Now take that sulky look off your face,
and let me put on your silver slippers. He
will be waiting so eagerly to meet you!'

7

'Then he can go on waiting!' said the
Princess. 'Anyway, the silver slippers
pinch!' And she kicked them off and ran
from the room. Then, she wriggled out of
her glittering gown, and put on one of
plain blue linen. This done, she tiptoed
down the back-stairs.

8

No one saw her slip quietly out of a side
door of the palace.

Prince Benedict whistled cheerfully as he marched along the road away from the town. 'This walking is thirsty work!' he said presently. And hearing the sound of running water, he turned off the road.

The stream was not far away, and, sitting on the bank beside it, was a girl in a blue linen dress. She was bathing one of her feet.

'Have you hurt it?' he asked.

She nodded. 'It's a blister, I think. I came away – well, in rather a hurry, and I forgot to put on sensible shoes.'

'Let me bandage it for you,' said Benedict. 'Where are you going?'

'I've no idea!' said the girl airily. 'As a matter of fact, I'm running away!'

Benedict sat back on his heels and laughed. 'I'm running away too!' he said. And then they both laughed. 'I've made up my mind to go out into the world and find adventures.'

'That's just what I thought of doing!' said the girl.

'But girls don't do that sort of thing!' said Benedict.

'Why shouldn't they?' she asked.

'All right,' said Benedict, 'let's go on together. What's your name? Mine is – er – er – John.'

'And mine is – is – Jane,' said the girl. And off they went, side by side.

13

Towards evening, she said suddenly:
'When we started out this morning, all
the carts and carriages were going this way
and that. Why are they all racing back to
the town now? And everyone is looking
behind them in a frightened sort of way!'
14

'Good gracious, I'd quite forgotten!'
said John. 'It's because of Giant
Grimblegraw. Sometimes after dusk he
comes prowling out of his great grim
castle. He's as tall as the Town Hall, they
say. Each foot is as big as a bath, and
his eyes whizz round like Catherine-
wheels. Anyone he catches outside the
city walls, is never seen again.'

'How horrid!' said Jane. 'Couldn't we
make it our first adventure to find out
what has happened to all those poor
people?'

15

Suddenly, as she spoke, without any warning a huge foot came down, wumf! pinning the skirt of her dress to the bank on which they were sitting.

'Help!' she cried in a frightened voice. 'It's the Giant!' John snatched up a stick and prodded the great foot.

'Don't do that, it tickles!' rumbled Grimblegraw.

'Why don't you look where you're going?' John shouted up at him.

'Because my eyes whizz round like Catherine-wheels, I can't see clearly down there. But aren't you frightened of me, like the other little mannikins? They all squealed and ran away! Of course I caught them in the end.'

As he stooped to peer at them,
Grimblegraw grabbed Jane and John, and
dropped them into his coat pocket, where
they landed in a tangle of arms and legs.

'Well, this is an adventure, and no
mistake!' said John, as they sorted
themselves out in the darkness. 'These
"mannikins" must be the poor people
who are never seen again!'

'I don't like being stuffed in someone's dusty old pocket,' said Jane.

'Nor do I,' said John, and he poked his head out and shouted, 'Hi! Grimblegraw! Can't you put us somewhere else? It's stuffy in here.'

18

The Giant began to laugh, till John and Jane were nearly deafened at the noise. 'The cheek of it!' he said at last. 'But I like your spirit. All right: you can sit on my shoulders if you like.'

And still laughing, Grimblegraw scooped them out of his pocket and sat them down, one on each side.

'Where are you taking us?' asked Jane.

'Where I've taken all the others. To my great grim castle. To cook and clean. With my whizzing eyes, I can't see to do it for myself.'

'Why don't you go and capture someone your own size?' asked John, indignantly.

'Because there's no one my size left,' said Grimblegraw sadly. 'When my ten tall brothers went off to see the world, they said I was no use, after the Wuthering Witch made my eyes whizz round like Catherine-wheels because I offended her.'

'Haven't you asked what to do to be un-bewitched?' asked Jane.

'I'm too scared,' said Grimblegraw. 'She is so terrible that anyone who looks her in the face is turned to stone.'

Presently they realised that what at first
they had thought was a towering great
cliff in front of them, was really the
Giant's castle. Grimblegraw took a huge
key from his other pocket, and unlocked
an enormous door.

It clanged behind them, and after striding down endless passages, they came to the Giant's kitchen. Everything in it was giant-size: chairs, tables, pots and kettles.

'Where are the mannikins?' asked Jane. Grimblegraw nodded towards the shelves on which you would expect to see cups and saucers. Instead, there were rows and rows of unhappy-looking people sitting with dangling legs.

'That's where I puts 'em when I'm out, so that they can't get down and escape. Mannikins!' roared the Giant. 'Here are two more of you, to take the place of the ones who got in the way when I stamped yesterday. Show 'em how you go about your jobs. I'm hungry! I want my supper!'

22

He put John and Jane down, and then
he fetched an enormous dustpan and
brush, swept the mannikins from the
shelves, and tipped them, helter skelter,
on the floor.

23

Some of them ran to roll out enormous carrots and turnips, which were cut up by two men using a giant-sized knife like a two-handled saw. The small pieces they piled into the bowls of several tablespoons, arranged see-saw fashion over a row of egg-cups.

This done, some of the others jumped smartly on the handles of the spoons so that the vegetables flew up in a curve and fell – plop! – into a cauldron of water boiling on the fire.

Some of them lugged out a tablecloth as large as a tennis court, and others bowled plates and cups from a cupboard.

And every now and then Grimblegraw would jump up and roar, 'Faster! Faster! Or I shall stamp!'

And with a cry of fear the mannikins would scuttle round even faster.

'That always gets 'em going,' said Grimblegraw. 'But the ones who get in the way when I stamp aren't any use any

more. They don't seem to be the right
shape somehow.'

'I'm not surprised,' said John.

'And then next day I have to go off and
hunt some more to take their place!'
went on Grimblegraw.

When the Giant had eaten supper, he
sat back and went to sleep in his chair. At
the first snore, the mannikins swarmed up
the wrinkles of his stockings, and
scrambled up on to the table any way they
could, where they gobbled up every
crumb they could find. John and Jane
joined them.

'Caught you today, did he?' said a
young man sitting on the edge of a plate,
licking his fingers. 'Poor things!'

'Can't you escape somehow?' asked
Jane.

'We've tried. But the locks and bolts are
all out of reach,' said the young man
sadly.

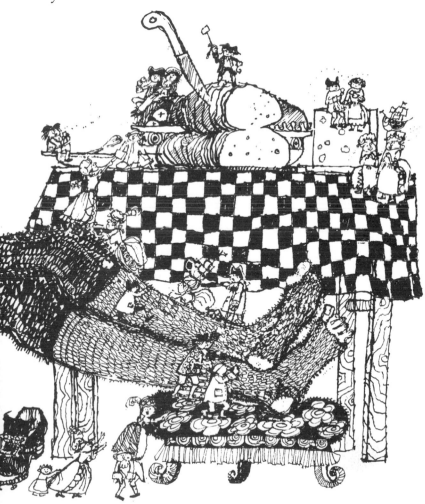

When they had been placed on the shelves for the night with the other mannikins, Jane whispered, 'If we could make the Wuthering Witch tell us how to stop Grimblegraw's eyes whizzing, he could let the mannikins go, and he wouldn't need to capture people any more.'

John nodded. 'But first we've got to escape from the castle.' He nudged the old woman sitting next to him. 'How does Grimblegraw know if any mannikins are missing, if his eyes are always whizzing round?'

'He weighs us every morning in his great kitchen-scales,' she replied. 'If the

weight is short, he goes off hunting for more of us. Now leave me alone, I want to go to sleep.'

Later that night, John and Jane woke the other mannikins, and explained the plan they had invented. In great excitement they all took off their belts and sashes and stockings. The women tore strips from their skirts and petticoats, and then they tied them all together into a long rope, and lowered John and Jane to the floor, who then climbed into the pocket of the sleeping giant and hauled the rope in after them.

'Good luck!' the mannikins whispered.

'Thunder and lightning!' roared Grimblegraw, when he weighed his prisoners next day. 'I'm two mannikins short again! I shall have to go out and hunt down a couple more!'

As he stumped off to the castle door, John and Jane tied the end of the rope to the button of his pocket flap, and as he turned to lock the great door behind him, they let it down, swarmed down to the ground and began to run.

They ran and ran until they reached a wide barren moor.

'Let's ask the old man standing over there if he can tell us the way to the Wuthering Witch,' said Jane. 'Why, it isn't a man: it's a statue!' she went on when they drew level with him.

'It isn't a statue,' said John, in an awed voice. 'It's a man who's been turned to stone, from his boots to his waistcoat buttons!'

'By the Wuthering Witch?' asked Jane.
John nodded. 'Let's ask at that cottage
over there how we can find her,' he said.

'The Wuthering Witch?' said the old
woman who opened the door to their
knock. 'Follow the stone people, my
dears. They will lead you to her cave by
the magic lake. All night she takes the
shape of a Snarling Beast, while she goes
about her wickedness. As the sun rises, she
leaves her cave and goes down to the lake.
When she plunges into its magic waters,
she turns back to her witch's shape. But
do not look at her terrible face when she
comes out, or you too will be turned to
stone!'

Although night had fallen, John and Jane set out once more. The moon light shone on more and more stone people, men, women, and even children.

Just as day was breaking, they came upon the dark mouth of the cave, and the glimmering waters of the lake. Safely hidden among the bushes growing at the mouth of the cave, they waited for the dawn.

As the sun began to rise, from the depths of the cave they heard a snarling, yarling sound. They shrank back into the bushes, not daring to look, but the snarling sound passed them, and grew fainter, as the Beast went down to the lake.

When it had gone by, Jane peered through her fingers. 'Look at the paw marks it has left in the sand! Let's follow them down to the lake, then we can ask our question when the Witch leaves the water, before she goes back to her cave!'

Shielding their eyes, they followed the paw marks down to the lake. Suddenly, there was a swirling of waves.

'She is coming! The Wuthering Witch!' cried John, and they crouched down on the sand.

As she passed them, she crooned, in a wuthering, wheedling voice: 'Look at me! Look at me!' But John and Jane only bowed their faces even lower, and followed the trail of her human footprints as she walked back to the cave.

'Wuthering Witch!' called John, with his head still bent. 'How can we cure the whizzing eyes of Giant Grimblegraw?'

'You have but to touch his eyelids with water from the magic lake,' she replied, in the same monotonous voice.

'Is that all?' cried Jane, starting up and clapping her hands. 'Oh, thank you – thank . . .' Her voice tailed off.

'Don't look up!' shouted John. But he was too late. Jane was already turned to stone. And the Witch had disappeared.

34

'Jane! Jane!' he cried. But of course she could not answer. He turned and shouted, 'Wicked, wicked Wuthering Witch! I don't care what happens to Grimblegraw and the mannikins if only you will make Jane alive again!' But the only answer was a low cackling laugh from the depths of the cave.

So he said to the statue which had been Jane: 'Don't despair! First, I shall take the magic water to Giant Grimblegraw. Then I will come back, and, somehow, I shall rescue you!'

He ran down to the lake, and filled one
of his shoes with the precious water.
'Poor, poor Jane! Before I go, I'll just say
goodbye,' he thought.

But just as he reached her, he stumbled
and fell, and the magic water splashed all
over her cold, grey feet. As he got up
again, he suddenly saw they were no
longer made of stone, and from her ankles
upwards slowly rose a tide of colour, until
at last her rosy cheeks bunched into a
wide smile. The spell was broken.

'Oh John!' she cried, 'However did you
do it?'

'It must have been the water from the

lake,' said John. 'Before we go, let's sprinkle it on all the stone people we can find!'

'But – the Wuthering Witch . . .?' began Jane.

'I don't think we need worry about her for a little,' said John. 'Listen!' From inside the cave came the unmistakable sound of snoring.

'Come on, before she wakes!'

They raced down to the lake, and each with a shoeful of water hurried from one statue to another. Splashed with the smallest drop, each one came to life, till there was not a stone figure left.

Then John and Jane said goodbye, and amid the cheers of the rescued people they set off across the moor, slowly and carefully, so that not a drop of the precious water should be spilt from the shoe.

When they reached the castle, Grimblegraw was just returning from his day's hunting. As he unlocked the great door, they slipped in at his heels.

As soon as he entered the kitchen, he roared, 'I've had no luck today, mannikins, so you'll have to work that much harder. Hurry, or I shall stamp!' And he lifted his great foot.

'Stop! Stop!' shouted John and Jane, 'We have just come back from the Wuthering Witch, and she has told us how to cure your poor whizzing eyes!'

'Now, sit down on the floor,' said John, 'and close your eyes.' There was a scuttling of mannikins to safety as he obeyed.

Then very carefully, lest the precious water should spill, they climbed up the Giant, passing the shoe from one to the other at the steepest places, using creases and buttonholes as footholds. Up they went, till at last they stood on the tangle of his bristling beard.

Then, standing on tiptoe, they touched
each of his huge eyelids with a finger
dipped in the magic water. This done they
scrambled down again.

'Now, open your eyes!' they shouted.
And like blinds lifting in a window his
great lids rose, and the whizzing of his
eyes grew slower and slower, until at last
they were still.

A wide smile spread across
Grimblegraw's face, and a cheer went up
from the watching mannikins.

42

'Tomorrow, I shall join my ten tall brothers,' said the Giant. 'I need you no longer, my little mannikins.' And he opened the great door to the outside world.

Singing and laughing, they trooped out, and away to their homes. But when the Giant returned to the kitchen, to his surprise he found John and Jane still there.

'What now, little people?' he said.
'Don't you want to go home too?'

'The trouble is this,' said John with a frown. 'If I go back, I shall have to marry that tiresome Princess Yolanda. And the only girl I want to marry is Jane.'

A slow smile spread over Jane's face. 'And the only person I want to marry is John. I suppose, by any chance, your name isn't really – Benedict?'

'However did you guess?' he answered in astonishment.

'Because *my* name is Yolanda! And all this time we thought we were running away from one another!'

And they began to laugh. When they explained the joke, Grimblegraw laughed with them, and they laughed till their sides ached.

Then the grateful Giant carried them
back to the town, and of course they were
married.

The people sang and danced in the
streets, and the bells rang until the slates
flew off the steeples. Everyone rejoiced.

But the ones who rejoiced most of all were Prince Benedict and Princess Yolanda.

Gemma and the Witch

Pamela Gilbert

Illustrated by Oonagh Don

A Witch

There were always plenty of witches in
Hodson Wood. Gemma had not actually
seen them, but she was quite sure that
they were there.

Early one morning she walked into the
wood at the end of the garden. It was a
grey, cloudy day and quite dark in the
wood. Gemma was not really afraid, but
she jumped when a squirrel scuttled
through the grass and up into the
branches of the chestnut tree.

'What are you doing in my wood?' the
voice seemed to come from the tree tops.

Gemma turned and then scampered
back down the path.

'Stop! Come back at once,' cried the
voice.

It was the sort of voice you obeyed,
even though you were scared. Gemma
crept slowly back up the path.

'That's better. Now I can see you
properly.'

As nothing terrible happened, Gemma
looked up into the branches of the
chestnut tree. And there was the witch!

Gemma knew that it was a witch but, if
it had not been for her high hat and her
long broomstick and her cat with green
eyes, she would not have been sure at all.

She looked more like one of the old
ladies who talked to her in the
supermarket. Her face was brown and
wrinkled like an apple which had been
stored too long and she looked so sad.

Suddenly Gemma was not frightened
any more. 'If I was a witch and could cast
spells and frighten people,' she said, 'I
would not be sad like you.'

6

The witch sighed a very long sigh. 'Things were very different when I was a young witch. I jumped on my broomstick and flew above the trees. I turned little boys into frogs and little girls into white mice. And everyone was frightened of me. But now I am so old and stiff that I can hardly climb on to my broomstick and I cannot remember any of my spells. So who's going to be frightened of me any more?'

'I was frightened,' said Gemma. 'I was so frightened that I ran away.'

'Yes, that was a nice change,' said the witch. 'It made me feel quite witch-like again. Now, if only I could think of some of my spells. Yesterday, I saw such a chubby little boy in the wood. He would have made a perfect, plump frog but, before I could think of the right boy-into-frog spell, he had gone. I feel so useless.'

8

'Perhaps you would find it easier to
remember nice spells,' said Gemma. 'I
can't see much use in turning little boys
into frogs, anyway.'

'I never thought of that,' said the witch.
'What kind of spells can you think of?'

Gemma thought a moment.

'Old Mrs Higgs next door is stiff and
full of aches like you. And she hasn't got a
broomstick to get about on either.
Couldn't you think of a spell to help her?'

The witch did not answer for several minutes . . . 'I'm beginning to remember some of the nice spells my mother taught me. And I haven't thought about them for years, being so busy with all the nasty

ones. . . . Yes, perhaps I could help this old lady of yours. I'll just fly along and have a look through her window.'

And she hopped on her broomstick, just as she used to do when she was a young witch, and flew off over the wood.

'Gemma,' called her mother. 'Where are you? . . . It's time for breakfast.'

'Do you know,' said Gemma as she went into the house. 'There's such a nice witch in Hodson Wood. She's going to help Mrs Higgs.'

'Yes dear,' said her mother. 'But do sit down and eat your cornflakes.'

And next door in the little house with bright red chimney pots, old Mrs Higgs was thinking about breakfast too. She climbed downstairs holding on to the banisters with both hands.

How stiff she was this morning! She felt like a clockwork doll that someone had forgotten to wind up.

The idea tickled Mrs Higgs and she laughed out loud. She always found plenty of things to laugh about.

'A hot cup of tea should set me up.' She always talked out loud, although there was no-one to hear her except Monty, her large tabby cat. Monty was quite used to such things and did not bother to open one eye.

'Might as well try some of my new rheumaticky pills Doctor gave me. . . .' Mrs Higgs swallowed two of the large, red pills and pulled a face.

Just at that moment the witch flew down and landed on the window-sill with her black cat. The window was open and there was a sudden cold blast of air.

Mrs Higgs pulled her striped yellow dressing-gown round her and took a gulp of tea.

The witch looked at her and thought that the black and yellow dressing-gown made her look like a caterpillar. She would have liked to turn her into one, but, as usual, she could not remember the spell.

So she rattled the window backwards and forwards and laughed. Mrs Higgs looked up to the ceiling and down to the floor.

'Silly old thing,' said the witch. 'She can't see me at all.'

Then Monty suddenly noticed the witch's cat perched on the end of the broomstick and spat.

Mrs Higgs looked at him in surprise.

14

This was not a bit like Monty. The
witch's cat put out her tongue at Monty
and he arched his back and spat again.

'Dear me,' said Mrs Higgs. 'That fish I
gave him last night couldn't have agreed
with him. Perhaps the rabbit would have
been better.'

She got up and walked very slowly to
close the window. All her bones creaked
like the springs of an old sofa.

The witch suddenly felt quite sorry for Mrs Higgs. 'And, after all, I did promise Gemma to help the old lady. I almost forgot.' She said this to her black cat Thunder, but Thunder was still glaring at Monty and took no notice.

The witch thought very hard and then the spell came to her as swiftly as the flight of a broomstick.

'Rheumaticky, rheumaticky, fly away rheumaticky. . . .'

She waved her arms towards Mrs Higgs, and Thunder, the cat, lifted up her head and howled. It was so long since the witch had remembered any of her spells that it gave her quite a shock.

Mrs Higgs had a peculiar feeling as though she wanted to skip round the room.

'Bless me,' she said to Monty. 'I do believe I feel much, much better. It must be the doctor's new rheumaticky pills. What marvellous things they are! I'll just put on my hat and coat and walk into town. It's a simply gorgeous day.'

And Mrs Higgs skipped up the stairs, two at a time.

'Well . . .' The witch looked up to the sky. 'Of all the ungrateful old women . . . pills indeed! Flashing thunder bolts!'

And the witch jumped on to her broomstick and flew off at such a pace that Thunder, the cat, had to cling on desperately with one paw.

They sailed high above Gemma's house
and on to Hodson Wood. Nobody
noticed them, not even Gemma, who was
just coming out of the house with her
mother. She was too busy swinging the
big, red shopping bag and thinking about
the things she was going to buy.

She followed her mother along the High Street and into the Post Office and General store, where Mr Soskins sold everything from baking dishes to bird seed. While her mother waited at the counter to buy some stamps, Gemma decided to spend her pocket money on lemon sherbets and chocolate whirls.

20

Then they went into the supermarket,
where Gemma plonked the large red
shopping bag on the trolley and pushed it
along behind her mother. She enjoyed
seeing how fast she could go with it,
without actually knocking anyone down.

'Be careful dear,' said her mother as she
stacked up with butter and cheese and
vegetables and tins of chicken mixture for
Jeremy, the labrador and pilchards for
Cluff, their large sandy cat. The trolley
was getting very heavy and Gemma could
not run with it any more.

Suddenly round the stacks of soup
came a bright, beaming face they knew. It
was Mrs Higgs, dressed in a big check
coat, which wrapped her up like a parcel,
and a bright yellow beret with a tassel.'

'Why, Mrs Higgs, how nice to see you out again. And looking so much better too!' said Gemma's mother.

Mrs Higgs beamed again, so that the whole of her face was one smile.

'You'll never believe it. Dr Pepper gave me some new pills ". . . well try them," he said "and see if they do any good." Large red ones, they are. And bless me, I only took two of them with my cup of tea and I feel a different creature. Quite like a young girl again.'

'How quite astonishing,' said Gemma's mother.

'But don't you see, it's not the pills at all,' cried Gemma. 'It's the witch. She said she could do it. Don't you remember?' She looked at her mother.

'What did you say, dearie?' Mrs Higgs looked puzzled.

'It's the witch who's cured all your aches and pains. The witch in Hodson

Wood.' Gemma rattled her trolley, as if a
loud noise would make it easier for Mrs
Higgs to understand.

'Gemma plays a lot in the woods, and I think she has met an old lady who tries natural cures,' explained Gemma's mother. 'She must have been talking to her about you.'

'That's very nice of you, Gemma, to think of me.' Mrs Higgs looked touched. 'And I expect it all helped to cure me, that and the doctor's pills, of course.'

Gemma's mother went on talking to Mrs Higgs, but Gemma pushed the trolley angrily round the corner past the soups.

How silly they both were. Couldn't they see that it was the witch who had done it, not the stupid pills? She must have visited Mrs Higgs specially and remembered the spell to do away with all aches and pains. And now the witch would be very angry. She might be so angry that she'd remember all her nasty spells and turn her mother and Mrs Higgs into frogs or cockroaches or something.

'Gemma,' called her mother. 'We're going home now. Push the trolley along to the check-out.'

Gemma swerved back round the corner and rattled the trolley at a rollicking pace towards the cashier's desk.

How she wished her mother would walk faster! She could hardly wait to get the shopping home and go out to find the witch.

As soon as her mother was busy in the kitchen, she tip-toed out of the house. Then she pushed open the garden gate and ran into Hodson Wood. It was splattering with rain, but the branches of the chestnut trees were so thick that she hardly felt it.

It grew darker and darker as she went
further into the wood and she could see
the eyes of the squirrels gleaming in the
branches.

30

Although she was expecting to see the witch, she still felt a bit nervous. And when she actually caught sight of her sitting on the same branch of the chestnut tree, she jumped three feet in the air. The witch sat there just as she had done before, with her tall hat, her long broomstick and her cat with green eyes. And she looked just as grumpy.

'So you've come.' The voice did not sound at all welcoming.

'Yes,' Gemma looked up very slowly. 'Did you think I wouldn't come to thank you? How clever of you to cure all Mrs Higgs' aches and pains!'

The witch snorted, so that the bough shook. 'Humph, I'm glad that someone knows who to thank. Mrs Higgs thinks that it's all due to the doctor's red pills. Anyone with any sense should know that it's magic.'

'She's very old, you know,' said

Gemma in her most soothing voice. 'You mustn't let it upset you. And after all, you did remember one of your spells, which proves that you really are a witch.'

The witch started to smile and then changed her mind. 'Yes, but it's not much use being a witch unless someone knows about it.'

'Well, I know,' said Gemma, 'and so does your cat.' Gemma looked up at Thunder, who stared back at her, her eyes as green as traffic lights at 'Go'.

'That's not the same at all,' said the
witch. 'I'd like everyone in the town to
know that I'm the witch and that what I
do is magic. Now suppose you arrange
something special, a spell that can be seen
by lots of people, not only Mrs Higgs.'

'I'm afraid that would be very difficult,'
said Gemma.

'Oh do try. You were so clever in thinking about Mrs Higgs.' The witch looked so hopeful that Gemma decided that she must think very hard indeed.

There was a long silence. The black cat closed her eyes and a squirrel came running down a branch of the chestnut tree to see why it was so quiet.

The witch sat looking at Gemma.

'I wonder . . . I wonder if it will work. . . .'

'You've thought of something . . .' the witch began.

'Well, it's only an idea,' said Gemma. 'But it's worth a try. Our lollipop lady, who helps us across the road outside the school, has left. And Councillor Bumble says that the town cannot afford to have another one. So all our mothers have asked if we can have a crossing instead, one with flashing lights. Then we can all cross the road safely again. But Councillor

34

Bumble says that's no use either. So do
you think you can cast a spell to give us a
crossing?'

'I really don't know. I've never tried
doing anything like that . . .'

Gemma jumped up and down. 'It
would be just the thing. If you come at
half past three, there would be crowds of
mothers outside the school and lots of
children too. And they would all see how
clever you are. Do come, please.'

'Well, I suppose if I think very hard and
look up all my old books of spells . . .'

'And then you'll come!' Gemma
skipped in the air. 'Tomorrow's the first
day of term, so everybody will be there.
And now I must run, or I'll be late for
tea.'

And all through tea and right up to bed
time, Gemma was very quiet. She was
too busy thinking about the witch and the
crossing and her marvellous idea.

'I hope you're not sickening for
something,' said her mother, 'or you'll
have to stay away from school
tomorrow.'

Gemma gasped. What an idea! Fancy
staying away from school and missing it
all.

So next morning she talked and asked even more questions than usual.

'Goodness me, what a chatterbox you are,' said her mother as she left her at the school gates.

Every other day Gemma enjoyed school, but today she could hardly wait until it was time to finish lessons. At last Mrs Lennard told them to clear away all the lumps of clay and pots of water they had been using for making farmhouses and trees.

She hurried to put on her coat and then remembered that she must go out slowly. It would never do to be so early that she missed the witch and all the excitement.

There was Miranda, who lived in the house just down the road from her.

'Oh, Gemma, do hurry up. I'm coming home with you,' she said.

But Gemma pretended not to hear. She took several minutes to change her shoes and put on her coat. Then she dawdled along the passage, pretending to look at the pictures.

'Come along, Gemma. Do you want to stay all night?' Mrs Lennard hurried her out of the front door.

Then she knew that she had been too slow, for all sorts of things were happening in the street. There were crowds of people outside the gate, mothers and children and a few policemen as well. She could not see her mother at all.

There was a peculiar smell as though
someone had let off a firework, and a thin
mist over the road. Gemma looked up
and saw a set of traffic lights larger than
she had ever seen before. It had a flashing
green light shining over the pavement, as
green as the eyes of Thunder, the cat. And
on top of the traffic lights sat the witch,
looking very pleased with herself.

None of the mothers and other children
seemed to have noticed the witch at all.
They were all staring down at a crossing
on the road, marked out by shiny silver
studs.

'How wonderful!' said one mother.
'We've really got our crossing at last. The
Department of Transport must have
realised how dangerous the road is for
children.'

'I am sure it's not them at all,' said another. 'It must be the students playing a practical joke.'

'And jolly good luck to them!' said Mr Beaver, the caretaker, coming up. 'It's about time somebody took the law into their own hands.'

'But, Mr Beaver, it's not the students at all,' cried Gemma. 'It's the witch. Can't you see her sitting on top of the traffic lights?'

Everybody then looked up at the traffic lights shining above them, but no-one except Gemma could see the witch at all.

'It's certainly very peculiar, though,' said another of the mothers, 'I'm quite sure that there was no crossing here when I came to fetch Thomas.'

'Oh there you are, Gemma,' called her mother. 'I couldn't find you anywhere.'

'Oh, isn't it exciting!' said Gemma, catching hold of her mother's hand to cross the road. 'It's all the witch's doing, you know. She gave us the crossing, not Mr Bumble or the students or anyone.'

Her mother smiled. 'I do believe you're right dear. . . . It must be magic.'

The witch laughed loudly, a laugh sounding like a rusty saw cutting wood. Then she and Thunder jumped on the broomstick and flew over the heads of them all.

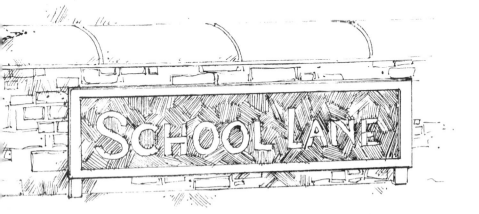

'What a cold wind!' said Gemma's
mother, clutching her coat collar. But
Gemma only laughed and waved as she
watched the broomstick turn and fly in
the direction of Hodson Wood.
Tomorrow she would go and see the
witch again.